BOOK 2

FiZZ and the DOG A...

For Rodney, Austin and Georgia. L.G.

For Rosie. S.M.K.

First American Edition 2017
Kane Miller, A Division of EDC Publishing

Text copyright © Lesley Gibbes, 2016
Illustrations copyright © Stephen Michael King, 2016
First published by Allen & Unwin Pty Ltd, Sydney, Australia

For information contact:
Kane Miller, A Division of EDC Publishing
PO Box 470663
Tulsa, OK 74147-0663
www.kanemiller.com
www.edcpub.com
www.usbornebooksandmore.com

Library of Congress Control Number: 2016944300

Printed in the United States of America
7 8 9 10
ISBN: 978-1-61067-613-7

FiZZ

and the
DOG ACADEMY
RESCUE

LESLEY
GIBBES

ILLUSTRATED BY
STEPHEN
MICHAEL
KING

Kane Miller
A DIVISION OF EDC PUBLISHING

Remi Razzle

Hunter

Sergeant Stern

Dr. Jabb

Apollo

Tom Whittaker

CONTENTS

With special thanks to Margaret Connolly, Sue Flockhart, Erica Wagner, Stephen Michael King and Trish Hayes.

L.G.

Chapter 1
It's Time to Go

"**Whoo-hoo!**" barked Fizz, as he leapt out of bed and raced to his breakfast bowl.

"Slow down, son," said Fizz's father. "There's plenty of time before you leave for the academy."

Fizz buzzed all over. His dream of becoming a police dog had come true.

"Did you clean your ears, sugarplum?" asked Fizz's mother.

"Yes, Mom," said Fizz, between mouthfuls of food.

"Well, give your fur a good shake. I want you to look especially fluffy on your first day of training."

"Yes, Mom," said Fizz, shaking till he looked like a white, fuzzy ball.

"Fancy my little Fizz training to be a police dog," she said.

"And not just any police dog," said Fizz's father, "but an *undercover* police dog. An undercover police dog doesn't have to *look* like a police dog."

"That's right, dear. No one will suspect our Fizz is a fierce undercover agent," said Fizz's mother, looking at him proudly.

Fizz pricked his ears. The deep rumbling of Tom Whittaker's pickup pulling up outside the Sunnyvale Boarding House for Dogs meant it was time to go.

"Tom's here!" said Fizz, wagging his fluffy tail and hoping for a quick good-bye. Tom was the groundskeeper and he had known Fizz since he was a pup.

4

"It's not too late to change your mind, sugarplum," said Fizz's mother. "Ms. Trunchon at the Dog Employment Department can always find you another job."

"I don't need Ms. Trunchon, Mom. I'm going to be an undercover police dog!" said Fizz.

"Well then," said Fizz's father, "we'll see you on graduation day."

Fizz ran out the door and jumped onto the front seat of Tom's pickup.

"Ready?" asked Tom.

"You bet I am!" said Fizz, wriggling with excitement.

Tom drove out the boarding house gate and headed for the Blue Haven Police Academy for Dogs.

"You did it, Fizz. You really did it!" said Tom, beeping his horn. "See, you don't know what you can do until you try!"

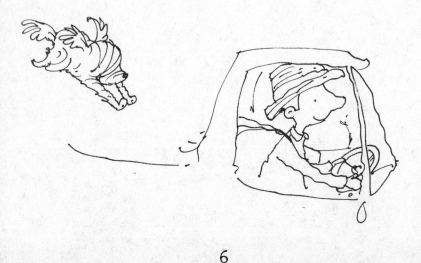

izz couldn't believe his eyes. The Blue Haven Police Academy for Dogs was enormous.

"These facilities are state-of-the-art," said Tom, as he parked at the entrance. Fizz's stomach fluttered with anticipation.

"Listen to your instructors and you'll be fine," said Tom, opening the door of the pickup. "I'll be back with your family on graduation day."

Tom gave Fizz a good-bye pat, then drove away.

Fizz looked over the academy grounds. The police dog tryouts had been hard, but training at the academy was going to be even harder.

He watched as dogs of all
shapes and sizes arrived.
A Great Dane was
squashed into the
front seat of a little

red car. A rottweiler slid off the back tray
of a green dump truck, and a bus with an
embarrassing advertisement for
dog-worming pills on the side
of it dropped off another three
trainee police dogs. And then a

graceful little dog arrived in a circus trailer.
Fizz stared as she pranced her way over to
the academy.

"Take a photo, sweetie, it will last longer," she said.

"Sorry," said Fizz. "It's just that I've never seen a dog like you before. What are you?"

"I'm a Chinese crested," she said, tossing her head. "My name's Remi Razzle. I'm a circus dog. What's your name?"

"My name's Fizz," he said, shaking the fur from his eyes.

Remi was the most unusual dog Fizz had ever seen. She had long silky hair on her head and tail and legs, but no hair at all on the rest of her body.

"I'm training to be an *undercover* police dog," said Remi, swishing her tail.

"So am I!" barked Fizz. He was relieved he wasn't the only small dog at the academy.

10

A police paddy wagon, with its sirens wailing, stopped to deliver another trainee dog. Out jumped an enormous midnight-black German shepherd. It was Amadeus. And behind him came his father, a powerful police dog.

"Listen carefully, son," said the police dog to Amadeus. "You are a Wolfgang, and Wolfgangs are always winners."

Amadeus stood up straight. His father leaned in closer.

"Every Wolfgang has taken the Top Dog Award on graduation day, and so will you! Don't let me down…or else!"

Fizz and Remi walked quickly past Amadeus. Fizz hoped Amadeus hadn't seen him. They had gone head-to-head at the police dog tryouts, and Amadeus was not happy that a little dog like Fizz had made it through to the academy for training.

"It's not too late to chicken out, Powder Puff!" called Amadeus, spotting Fizz's fuzzy coat. "You're in Wolfgang territory now!"

Chapter 3

The Vet Check

izz and Remi assembled with Amadeus and the other trainee dogs in the quadrangle at the center of the academy. At one end was a speaker's podium, and standing at the podium in his smart blue uniform was Sergeant Stern.

"Attention, please!" he called. "My name is Sergeant Stern and I'm your training officer here at the academy. As some of you may know, I'm the sergeant at Sunnyvale City Police Station. However, as the regular training officer is ill, I've been asked to take his place."

Fizz breathed easier and the butterflies in his stomach settled. He was glad to see Sergeant Stern's familiar face.

"Over the coming weeks you will be trained in four key areas: agility, scent, search and attack. You must reach a high level of ability in each area to become a police dog. Those of you training to become undercover police dogs" – Sergeant Stern looked at Fizz and Remi – "will have an additional challenge."

Fizz got goose bumps.

What might the challenge be?

"You must all be congratulated for making it this far," continued Sergeant Stern. "But there is a waiting list of dogs ready to take your place should you find the training too difficult, or if you cannot continue due to accident or illness."

Amadeus turned to Fizz. "You'll get replaced after the first obstacle course, Powder Puff."

Fizz knew that if he didn't do well at training he'd be sent to Ms. Trunchon. And if he was sent to Ms. Trunchon, she'd give him a horrible job like advertising worming pills on the side of a bus.

"Your first day will start with a vet check, followed by a tour of the academy," said Sergeant Stern. "You'll then be shown

to your rooms. Dinner is in the dining hall each evening at dusk. This way, please."

Fizz, Remi, Amadeus and all the other dogs followed Sergeant Stern to the veterinary office and formed a line outside.

"Dogs before fur balls!" said Amadeus, pushing in front of Fizz and stepping on his paw. It was still sore from the tryouts.

"This is Dr. Jabb, our veterinarian at the academy, and her assistant dog Shamus," said Sergeant Stern.

Shamus was a large rottweiler. He had a tuft of orange fur on the top of his head and an unfortunate habit of spitting when he talked.

"Dr. Jabb will give you a thorough examination to make sure you're fit and healthy. If you don't pass your vet check, you're out. I'll leave you in Dr. Jabb's capable hands," said Sergeant Stern.

"This way, pleassssse," spat Shamus, ushering the first three dogs into the waiting room.

"Say it, don't spray it," jeered Amadeus, making the other dogs laugh at Shamus.

Fizz watched as three dogs went into the exam room for their examination. A short time later only two dogs came out.

"What happened?" asked Fizz.

"The dalmatian has ingrown toenails. He has to see Ms. Trunchon for a more suitable job," said Shamus, sounding a little pleased. "You're next!"

Fizz's throat tightened. He was well, but his paw was tender. He hoped it wouldn't be a problem.

Fizz, Remi and Amadeus filed inside.

"What's your name, dear?" asked Dr. Jabb, snapping on a pair of rubber gloves.

"Remi Razzle, doctor," said Remi, leaping up onto the examination table and holding a handstand before sitting down.

"Ssshow off!" said Shamus, spraying dog biscuit crumbs all over Fizz.

Dr. Jabb gave Remi a thorough check. "You're in perfect health, dear," she said, reaching into a striped box. "You may have a biscuit treat before you go."

Fizz was next.

"What's your name, dear?" asked Dr. Jabb.

"Fizz," he said, hopping onto a chair then up to the examination table.

"Sorry dear, what was that?" asked Dr. Jabb.

"Fuzz," barked Amadeus, before Fizz could answer.

"Right, Fuzz," said Dr. Jabb. "There's nothing to worry about. Stand still, please."

Amadeus howled with laughter.

"My name's Fizz, Dr. Jabb," said Fizz, standing as still as possible.

Dr. Jabb poked and prodded. Then she lifted up his sore paw and paused. Fizz was sure she'd found something she didn't like.

"You're in great shape, Fizz. You may have a biscuit treat too."

Fizz breathed easier and got down.

"Wait, Dr. Jabb," barked Amadeus. "Fuzz's got black things in his fur!"

"What, fleas?" cried Dr. Jabb, quickly searching through Fizz's coat.

"I *haven't* got fleas, Dr. Jabb," said Fizz.

"We can't take a chance with a flea outbreak at the academy," said Dr. Jabb.

"You'll need a flea bath immediately. Shamus, bring me a new bottle of flea treatment, and be careful to hold it gently in your jaw. I'm finding your teeth marks on all my bottles and boxes."

"Can't we just send him home?" asked Shamus.

Fizz held his breath.

"No, Shamus, and it's not nice to be so pleased at others' misfortunes."

"Phew!" sighed Fizz. He'd passed the vet check!

Amadeus was rolling on the floor in hysterics.

"I wouldn't be laughing too hard, dear," said Dr. Jabb, reading Amadeus's medical file. "You're due for your parvovirus vaccination!"

Chapter 4
The Challenge

Fizz ate breakfast early the next morning. He was too excited to sleep. Sergeant Stern had called everyone to the agility course for their first training session and he didn't want to be late.

"Wait for me!" called Remi, racing to catch him. "Did you hear what happened to Wesley last night? Someone swapped his food bowl and he had fried liver instead of boiled chicken. He had an allergic reaction and had to go home. The cook's furious. She'd bought four weeks' worth of food especially for him. That's two dogs who have been sent home and we haven't even had our first training session!"

"You mean three dogs," said Fizz. "Someone stole Lucinda's squeaky toy last night. She was so frantic Sergeant Stern told her to go home. He had thought she was good enough to take the Top Dog Award this year."

"Out of my way, losers," said Amadeus, shoving past Fizz and Remi. "The only Top Dog around here is me!"

Fizz and Remi joined Sergeant Stern and the other trainee police dogs in front of the agility course, which was a track laid out with obstacles along it.

"This morning we're going to work on your coordination, strength and stamina," he said.

Fizz's heart pounded in his chest. The agility course looked challenging.

"Fizz will go first, followed by Apollo," said Sergeant Stern. "Take care on the balance beam, it's trickier than it looks."

Fizz stepped up to the starting line.
He could see the high balance beam in the
center of the course.

"Ready?" asked Sergeant Stern.
Fizz nodded. "Go!"

Fizz sprang over the first two
jumps, then weaved in and out of a set
of posts, sending clumps of grass flying.
He raced through a cloth tunnel, jumped
through a set of hoops and ran up and over
a seesaw. His muscles tensed. The balance
beam was ahead. He climbed up onto the
high platform and paused.

"He's chicken. Too scared to cross," jeered Amadeus.

Fizz's heart raced, but he stepped carefully onto the balance beam. The beam wobbled under his feet. Fizz caught his breath, then tiptoed step-by-step across the shaky beam.

"You made it, Fizz!" cheered Remi, standing on her back legs and stepping in a circle.

Fizz raced down the ramp, scrambled over a set of slippery barrels and skidded down a slide to the finish line, in front of Sergeant Stern.

"Good work, Fizz," said Sergeant Stern.

Apollo the Doberman was next. Fizz watched as he bounded onto the balance beam and took some wobbly steps.

"He's going to topple," cried Amadeus. "For sure!"

The balance beam shook and quivered.

"Come on, Apollo, you can do it!" barked Remi.

Then, with a crack and a yelp, Apollo and the balance beam crashed to the ground.

"He's hurt!" called Fizz, running over to help. "Look, he's twisted his ankle."

Sergeant Stern inspected Apollo's leg and the broken balance beam. "It looks like you'll be going home, Apollo. Your ankle is too swollen to continue training."

Sergeant Stern helped Apollo to his feet. "Amadeus, walk Apollo slowly to the vet so Dr. Jabb can strap his leg. Sorry, everyone, but that's it for the agility course today. We'll continue your stamina training on the exercise tracks and swimming pool. Fizz and Remi, I'd like you to stay behind for some undercover training please."

Fizz's legs shook like jelly. Remi bounded over enthusiastically.

Sergeant Stern clasped his hands behind his back. "Every year, the undercover dogs are given a special challenge to test their detective skills. Fizz, Remi, your challenge is to solve a mystery. Four trainee police dogs have been sent home and replaced with dogs from the waiting list. I don't believe they're all accidents. I want you to find out who's doing this and why. Solve the mystery, and you'll pass your undercover training. Fail, and you won't graduate to become undercover police dogs."

Fizz gulped.

"Start by investigating the balance beam," said Sergeant Stern, before he turned and headed off for the exercise tracks.

Fizz and Remi inspected the balance beam together.

"Look," said Remi. "Someone's chewed the bottom of the balance beam support, and they've dug around the base to make sure it would topple."

"Sergeant Stern's right," said Fizz, narrowing his eyes. "This is no accident. This is sabotage! Someone switched Wesley's food bowl on purpose, someone hid Lucinda's squeaky toy, and someone sabotaged the agility equipment today."

"But who?" asked Remi.

"Who has the most to gain if the best dogs are sent home?" asked Fizz. "Who has to win Top Dog or else? Amadeus!"

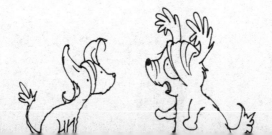

Chapter 5

The Clue

"If it is Amadeus, we're going to need proof," said Fizz, pacing up and down in his room. "Did you notice anything strange about the bite marks on the balance beam?"

"They were large," said Remi. "It has to be a big dog, about the size of Amadeus."

"But most of the dogs at the academy are big," said Fizz, shaking his head. "We need something else."

"What about the bite pattern?" said Remi. "There's a gap in the bite marks like teeth are missing."

"That's it, Remi!" said Fizz. "If we can match the bite pattern from the balance beam to the bite pattern of a dog at the academy, then we've found our saboteur."

"But how?" asked Remi.

"Chew toys!" cried Fizz, jumping up and down. "Come on, let's check the chew toys while everyone's at the tracks."

Fizz and Remi tiptoed down the hall and inspected the chew toys, room by room.

"None of the bite marks match, not even close," said Remi, her tail drooping.

"But we haven't checked Amadeus's room yet," said Fizz. "Can you see his chew toy?"

Remi searched furiously. "There's nothing here," she said, rummaging through Amadeus's basket. "He hasn't got one. We need more clues or we won't solve the mystery. And we *have* to pass our undercover training."

"And pass the regular police dog instruction too," said Fizz. "Let's meet up after search training today."

Fizz and Remi left the boarding house and made their way to the academy's bushland reserve. Sergeant Stern was waiting in a clearing with a large canvas bag.

"This afternoon, you're going to learn how to track by scent. A police dog must have a keen sense of smell and be able to follow a scent trail. I have hidden items of clothing in the bush for you to find. You will each sniff an item of clothing and find its missing pair by scent. There's a five-minute time limit for you to find your item and bring it back."

Sergeant Stern placed a shoe, sock or glove in front of every dog to sniff.

Fizz sniffed a shoe. His nose tingled as the scent of stinky cheese filled his nostrils.

"Get ready," said Sergeant Stern. "Go!"

Fizz sniffed the ground until he found the right scent. Then he followed the scent trail off into the bush. The bush was rugged and dense and the trail wasn't easy to follow.

"Out of my way, Powder Puff," said Amadeus, bumping Fizz into a prickle bush. "You couldn't find a liver treat in a pet shop."

Fizz scrambled to his feet. His shoulder stung with prickles, but Fizz wasn't going to let Amadeus get the better of him. He took a deep sniff and found his scent trail.

"Three minutes to go," called Sergeant Stern.

The scent trail was getting stronger and Fizz knew he was close. His nose twitched. He had the cheesy smell, but he couldn't see the shoe.

"Two minutes," called Sergeant Stern.

Fizz searched frantically, then he shook the fur from his eyes and looked up. The gym shoe was dangling from a tree. Fizz jumped for the shoe, but it was out of his reach.

Amadeus ran past with a glove in his mouth. "Even your girlfriend has found her sock, slowpoke!"

As he brushed past the tree, the shoelace dangled free. Fizz jumped and snapped at it.

Got it! Quick as lightning, Fizz turned and ran.

"Thirty seconds remaining," called
Sergeant Stern.

Fizz's feet pounded over rocks and dirt.
He heard the other dogs chanting.

"Ten, nine, eight, seven, six, five, four,
three, two, one…"

He skidded into the clearing in front
of Sergeant Stern just before he called,
"Time's up!"

Fizz was panting hard.

"I didn't think you were going to make it. What happened?" asked Remi.

"Someone's been moving the clothing. My shoe was up a tree. Did everyone make it back?" asked Fizz.

"No, Hunter didn't make it," said Remi. "I think he could be in trouble. Come on, we've got to find him."

Fizz and Remi raced into the bush and picked up Hunter's scent trail. Then a terrible yelp of pain echoed through the bush. Fizz and Remi ran to the sound.

"Over here!" cried Fizz.

Hunter was lying in a patch of stinging nettles with a sock in his mouth. He was covered in painful bumps and welts.

"Sergeant Stern would never have hidden the sock in a patch of stinging nettles," said Fizz. "Someone did this on purpose!"

Fizz heard a rustle in the bushes. It was Sergeant Stern.

"Hunter, you poor fellow, those stinging nettle welts look serious," he said. "I'm sorry, but you'll have to go home."

Hunter dropped the sock from his mouth and howled in disappointment.

As Sergeant Stern carried Hunter off
to the vet, Fizz looked at the sock on the
ground. His skin prickled. "Remi, I've found
a clue! Look there's a hair."

"Midnight black? Amadeus?" asked Remi.

"No," said Fizz, puzzled. "It's orange."

Chapter 6

6

Guess that Scent

"Orange?" said Remi at breakfast the next morning. "How can the hair be orange? No trainee police dog has orange hair. Maybe Amadeus planted it there to throw us off the scent."

"Maybe," said Fizz, staring into the distance. "But one thing's for sure, we've got to solve this mystery before anyone else gets hurt."

Sergeant Stern appeared at the dining hall door. "Finish your breakfast and meet me in the quadrangle for training. We're going to start the day with a game I like to call, Guess that Scent."

46

Sergeant Stern had arranged four small boxes on a low table.

"The aim of the game is to guess what's in the box by using your sense of smell. Remi, you may go first," said Sergeant Stern.

Remi trotted forward and smelled the first box.

"Chocolate," she said.

"Very good, Remi," said Sergeant Stern. "Now the other boxes?"

"Peanut butter, sunscreen and…soap?" said Remi.

"Close, the last box was talcum powder," said Sergeant Stern, putting out four new boxes. "Your turn, Amadeus."

Amadeus strutted up to the table. "Watch and learn, Powder Puff," he growled in Fizz's ear. "Too easy. That's bubble gum, fertilizer, broccoli and basil – actually, purple basil, Sergeant Stern."

"Excellent, Amadeus. Molly, your turn."

Molly was a golden retriever with a good nose for food. "Baked beans, cinnamon, strawberry and…" Molly sniffed the last box. Her eyes bulged and her nose turned red. She shook her head violently and sneezed.

Sergeant Stern opened the fourth box. "Crushed chili pepper!" he cried in disbelief. Sergeant Stern fetched a cold cloth and wiped Molly's nose.

Fizz checked out the box. Stinging red-hot chili peppers.

"Fizz, take Molly to the vet. The chili peppers have burned her nose. The rest of you can practice your attack skills in the recreation hall."

Fizz walked Molly to the vet, where Dr. Jabb examined her nose.

"Is she going home?" asked Shamus, who was playing with a pink squeaky toy.

"Yes, Shamus, and will you please put that toy away. I can't think with all that squeaking!"

Sergeant Stern arrived to check on Molly. Dr. Jabb was putting burn cream on her nose.

"Perhaps it's time to get a guard dog, Sergeant Stern," suggested Dr. Jabb. She had a brochure with a picture of a fierce red ridgeback on the front.

"Guard dogs for hire," read Sergeant Stern.

Fizz recognized the dog. It was Razor! *The perfect job for him*, thought Fizz.

"I don't think that will be necessary," said Sergeant Stern.

"Six dogs sent home and six dogs from the waiting list called in to replace them. You'll be calling Shamus next, heaven forbid," said Dr. Jabb.

Shamus made a loud slurping noise as he chewed a treat.

"Shamus, will you stop eating all my treats!" said Dr. Jabb. "You've already lost three front teeth. Too many biscuits are not a good thing. Here, Fizz, take the treat box and share it with the other trainee dogs. I'm sure they're in need of a pick-me-up about now."

Dr. Jabb looked at Sergeant Stern.

"I'm very worried about the safety of my Shamus and the other dogs."

"I know. But I have every confidence our trainee undercover police dogs will get to the bottom of the matter," said Sergeant Stern, giving Fizz a look as he left.

Fizz gulped. He had no new clues and he wasn't any closer to solving the mystery.

Chapter 7

The Rescue

That night, Fizz dreamed about Wesley choking on fried liver and Apollo crashing from the balance beam. He heard again Hunter's agonized howl and the irritating squeak, squeak, squeak of Lucinda's chew toy. He tossed and turned in his basket as the smell of dog treats filled his nose, and Dr. Jabb said over and over, "You'll be calling Shamus next!"

"Wake up, Fizz! Wake up, it's morning!" said Remi. "Are you all right? You sounded like you were having a nightmare."

"I think I ate too many treats."

Fizz looked at the treat
box beside his basket. His
eyes traced around the curve
of a bite mark.

"That's it!" he said, jumping
out of bed, tail wagging.
"I know who did it! It's been
staring me in the face all night.
This box is the missing clue!"

Remi looked at the bite
pattern on the box: a row of teeth, then a
gap where teeth were missing, then more
teeth marks. "They're a perfect match to
the bite marks on the balance beam! Is it
Amadeus?" asked Remi.

"No!" said Fizz. "Not Amadeus! It's
Shamus! He's the saboteur!"

Fizz paced up and down the room, putting the clues together. "Shamus spits when he talks because he has missing teeth. His bite pattern matches the bite marks on the balance beam. And the hair on the sock, Remi? Orange! Who has a patch of orange hair on the top of his head?

"Shamus knew Wesley was allergic to liver," Fizz went on. "He would have heard that when Wesley had his vet check."

Remi bounced on tiptoes. "Shamus was always so pleased when someone was sent home!"

"I bet his new pink
squeaky toy is the one
stolen from Lucinda!
And yesterday," said
Fizz, "I heard Dr. Jabb say
that it wouldn't be long before Sergeant
Stern called Shamus in as a replacement.
That means Shamus is on the waiting list.
Shamus wants dogs to be sent home so he
can be called up!"

Fizz raced to the door. "Come on, Remi,
we've got to stop Shamus before he makes
more trouble. We'll check the large
obstacle course first. That's where
we'll be training this morning,
and *that's* where Shamus will be
up to mischief!"

Fizz and Remi ran out of the boarding house and headed for the obstacle course.

"Can you hear that?" said Fizz, his ears pricking.

"Help! Pleassse help me!"

"It's Shamus!" said Remi. "He's in trouble." Fizz and Remi raced down the hill.

Shamus was on the rope suspension bridge, with his back legs dangling over the mud pit below.

"We've caught him red-handed," yelled Fizz. "He's been tricked by his own sabotage. Look, he's chewed through one of the ropes and now he's tangled in it!"

"Help," wailed Shamus. "The rope's ssslipping!"

"This is serious," said Remi. "We need help fast."

"Find Sergeant Stern and tell him what's happened," said Fizz. "We're going to need the rescue squad. Hurry!"

Remi raced away at full speed.

"The ropes are ssslipping!" cried Shamus, dropping lower and lower over the mud pit. "I can't ssswim, Fizz!"

Quick as a flea, Fizz climbed the ramp to the top of the wooden tower and tiptoed across the suspension bridge. He grabbed the end of the broken rope and pulled with all his might. If he let go, Shamus would fall into the deep mud.

Fizz held the rope with all his strength. Then he heard a wailing siren and saw the rescue truck speeding down the hill towards him. Out jumped Sergeant Stern and Remi, followed by two rescue squad officers and a Labrador. The chocolate-brown Labrador was wearing a red vest that said "trainee rescue dog" in fluorescent-yellow letters. Benny!

"Right, Benny, I want you up there helping Fizz to hold the rope. When I give you the signal, I want you to let Shamus drop safely onto the jump blanket. Have you got that?"

"Yes, sir," barked Benny.

Remi, Sergeant Stern and the two rescue officers stretched the jump blanket over the mud pit.

"Ready, Fizz and Benny? Go!"

Fizz and Benny let go together. Shamus slipped out of the ropes and plopped down onto the jump blanket. He crawled sheepishly over to Sergeant Stern.

"You have a lot of explaining to do, Shamus.
If Fizz and Remi hadn't found you, you would
still be dangling from the suspension bridge. Go
straight to my office and wait for me. This time
it's *your* turn to go home!"

Shamus trudged
slowly up the hill, his tail
between his legs.

Sergeant Stern turned to Fizz and Remi.

"Excellent job, you two. You solved the
mystery and proved that you qualify to be
undercover police dogs."

Remi did a circus backflip, and Fizz
buzzed with pride.

"Congratulations, Fizz!" cried Benny,
wagging his tail like a flag in
the wind. "You're
a *real* undercover police
dog now!"

Chapter 8

Graduation Day

izz, Remi, Amadeus and all the graduating police dogs had each received their official Police Dog Badge at the graduation ceremony. They were lined up waiting to find out who would be awarded Top Dog.

Fizz could see Tom and his family sitting in the front row.

"Every year the very best graduating dog is given the prestigious Top Dog Award," said Sergeant Stern. "However, this year, we have *two* winning dogs who will share the award."

Amadeus clenched his teeth. He had no intention of sharing *his* award.

"Our Top Dogs this year are…" announced Sergeant Stern, "Amadeus, for outstanding skills and superior physical strength…"

Amadeus leapt onto the stage and gave a loud, boastful victory howl. His father stood tall and proud.

"And," continued Sergeant Stern, "for excellent detective work, quick thinking and bravery… Fizz!"

Fizz stepped up and Sergeant Stern pinned the Top Dog Badge next to his Police Badge on the leather pouch around his neck.

"Well done, Amadeus, and well done, Fizz," said Sergeant Stern. "I expect to see you both bright and early at the Sunnyvale City Police Station on Monday."

Amadeus glared down at Fizz.

"Just keep out of my way and leave the real police work to me, Powder Puff!" Then he swatted Fizz with his tail and left.

Fizz's family raced to congratulate him. Bella, Puff-Pup, Fluff-Pup and Crystal gave him a happy group hug.

"Well done, son," said Fizz's father. "You've made me so proud."

"You'll always be my top dog, sugarplum!" said Fizz's mother.

Tom knelt down beside Fizz. "Congratulations!" he said, patting him firmly on the back. "I knew you could do it!"

It was time for the visitors and graduating dogs to leave the academy. Fizz and Remi stood at the gate and said their good-byes. A bus pulled up and several graduating dogs and their families boarded.

"Aren't you glad you're an undercover police dog and not the dog advertising charcoal pills for problem flatulence?" " asked Remi.

Fizz looked at the dog in the photo on the side of the bus. It was Bruno!

"What's flatulence?" asked Fizz.

"Wind," said Remi.

"What?" asked Fizz.

"Oh, don't make me say it, Fizz. Farts! Charcoal pills are for dogs who fart!"

And Fizz and Remi roared with laughter.